Science Un-fair!

The third and fourth graders marched excitedly into the auditorium for the science-fair judging.

"Wait quietly beside your exhibits, please," Ms. Vaughn, the principal, said.

Frank went to stand at the table beside his fingerprints project. Brett Marks walked past him. Suddenly Brett froze. "Oh no! I don't believe it!" he yelled. "After all my hard work. It's ruined."

Everyone turned to look. Brett's seismograph was lying smashed to pieces, half on the table, half on the floor. Next to it Mike Mendez's burglar alarm also lay smashed. Who could have done such a terrible thing?

The Hardy Boys® are: The Clues Brothers™

Available from MINSTREL Books

The Hardy Boys® are:

THE CLUES BROTHERS™

14

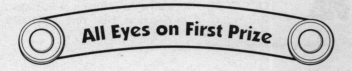

All Eyes on First Prize

Franklin W. Dixon

Illustrated by
Marcy Ramsey

A
MINSTREL®
BOOK

Published by POCKET BOOKS
New York London Toronto Sydney Tokyo Singapore

This book is a work of fiction. Names, characters, places and incidents are products of the author's imagination or are used fictitiously. Any resemblance to actual events or locales or persons living or dead is entirely coincidental.

A MINSTREL PAPERBACK *Original*

 A Minstrel Book published by
POCKET BOOKS, a division of Simon & Schuster Inc.
1230 Avenue of the Americas, New York, NY 10020

Copyright © 1999 by Simon & Schuster Inc.

ISBN: 0-671-03253-4

First Minstrel Books printing August 1999

10 9 8 7 6 5 4 3 2

FRANK AND JOE HARDY: THE CLUES BROTHERS is a trademark of Simon & Schuster Inc.

THE HARDY BOYS, A MINSTREL BOOK, and colophon are registered trademarks of Simon & Schuster Inc.

Cover art by Thompson Studio

Printed in the U.S.A.

QBP/✷

All Eyes on First Prize

1

Disaster Area

It was a blustery Monday morning at Bayport Elementary School. Frank Hardy sat near the back of the classroom beside his friend Chet Morton.

"How long to recess?" Chet whispered to Frank.

Frank looked surprised. "We only just got here, Chet."

"I know, but I'm starving."

Frank grinned. "You know your problem?" he whispered back. "You live for food!"

1

Chet pretended to be surprised. "What else is there?"

"Listen up, fourth graders," Mrs. Burton said. "I've got some important news for you. Two pieces of news, in fact."

The class looked up.

"I hope it's good news, like extra recess," Chet Morton whispered to Frank. "Not bad news like an extra math test."

"The first piece of news is that a new student will be joining us today," Mrs. Burton said. "His name is Billy Magee, and he has just moved here from California. So please make him feel welcome."

"Sure, we'll make him feel welcome, won't we?" Zack Jackson grinned at his friend Brett Marks. Zack was known as the class bully.

Frank saw Zack's mean look. He hoped the new kid wasn't a shrimp. Zack loved picking on little kids.

"Billy is still in the office with his mother, filling out forms," Mrs. Burton went on. "He'll be here shortly. But I'm going to go ahead and tell you the other important piece of news. We're going to have a science fair."

"Yeah!" The class was really interested now.

Chrissy Parker in the front row raised her hand. "For the whole school?" she asked. "The big kids always win."

Mrs. Burton shook her head. "This time it's just for the third and fourth graders. You have two weeks to make your projects. Then they'll be on display in the auditorium. They'll remain on display until the open house next month so that your parents can see them, too."

"Will there be prizes?" Brett asked.

Mrs. Burton smiled. "A store called the Nature Place has generously donated a gift certificate for the first prize. There will be ribbons for the other awards."

"Big deal," Zack muttered to Brett.

"The Nature Place is cool," Brett answered. "I'll just have to win first prize."

"I wonder if I could invent a new food," Chet said thoughtfully. "Something that

3

tasted good, filled you up, and had no calories."

"We have it already. It's called water, Chet," Frank answered.

At that moment the door opened and a boy came in. Frank thought that he must be a fifth or sixth grader. He was bigger than all the other kids in the classroom. He had red hair and a lot of freckles. Just then his face was bright red, too.

"Yes? Can I help you?" Mrs. Burton asked.

"I—I think I'm supposed to be here," the boy stammered. "I just moved here."

"You're Billy Magee?" Mrs. Burton sounded surprised.

The boy nodded.

Mrs. Burton smiled and held out her hand to him. "Welcome to our class, Billy. Let's see if we can find a seat for you." She looked around the classroom. "Ah, yes. There's a spare desk at the back of the room, next to Frank."

Frank waved and pointed to the empty

4

seat beside him. Billy started down the aisle toward his seat. As he passed Chrissy Parker's desk he sent a stack of papers flying.

"Whoops, sorry," Billy said. He turned around, and crash! His book bag knocked a pile of books onto the floor.

"I didn't mean to—" he began to say. He bent to pick up the books. There was a clatter as a pencil box fell to the floor. Pencils and pens rolled everywhere. The fourth graders were giggling.

"I think maybe you should sit down, Billy," Mrs. Burton said kindly. "Don't worry. Relax. Everyone is nervous on their first day."

Billy made it safely down the rest of the aisle. He went to sit down and knocked over his chair.

Zack Jackson was sitting on the other side of Billy. "Hey, Billy," he yelled. "You know how we can tell that you come from California? You're a walking earthquake!"

This made the whole class burst out laughing. Billy's face turned even redder.

Frank could see how embarrassed Billy was feeling.

"That wasn't nice, Zack," Mrs. Burton said quickly. "Imagine how you'd feel on your first day at a new school."

"I wouldn't destroy the classroom like Godzilla," Zack muttered to Brett. "Come to think of it, he looks like Godzilla, doesn't he?"

Brett chuckled.

Frank remembered how Zack had loved to tease him when he first moved to Bayport. He decided to be nice to Billy.

At recess Frank waited for Billy to come out to the schoolyard. "Hi, I'm Frank," he said. "Don't mind Zack. He's a pain. The other kids are nice. Come and meet my friend Chet."

Even Chet looked small beside Billy. "Hi," he said. "Do you want to share my chips?"

"Thanks, but I've got my own," Billy said. He pulled an identical pack of chips from his jacket pocket.

Chet's face lit up. "You like the same chips as me! Nacho cheese flavor!"

"Never go anywhere without them," Billy said. "I always keep a snack handy, especially Nacho cheese chips."

"Me, too!" Chet said. "I chose a jacket with extra big pockets so that I could always have a snack with me."

"What a great idea," Billy said. "Back in California we were big football fans of the Oakland Raiders. My big brother bought me this Oakland Raiders jacket. Maybe my mom could sew me extra pockets inside it."

They laughed.

"Hey, Frank, this guy's okay." Chet slapped Billy on the back.

"You want to play kickball with us?" Frank asked Billy. He headed for a group of fourth graders.

Frank's younger brother, Joe, was shooting hoops as they passed. "Hey, you guys," he called. "Did you hear about the science fair yet?"

"Mrs. Burton told us this morning,"

Frank answered. "I think I've got a great idea already."

"Me, too," Joe said. "I think I've got the best idea."

"Did you hear that the first prize is a gift certificate to that store called the Nature Place?" Mike Mendez, Joe's friend, joined them. "Isn't that cool? They have the best stuff in there."

"You just might win, Mike," Joe said. "You make great inventions."

"Yeah, but we're competing against fourth graders," Mike said. "It will have to be something totally awesome to win."

They went back to shooting hoops as Frank walked on with Chet and Billy. The kickball game hadn't started yet. Two captains were still picking teams.

"We're playing, too," Frank called.

"Okay, you guys can be on my team," a boy from the other fourth-grade class said. "We could use some boot power."

"What about earthquake power?" Zack taunted.

"Cut it out, Zack," Frank warned. He stood in line to kick the ball.

"I hope Mrs. Burton gives us plenty of time in the library today to research our science projects," Chet said. "I'm not too great about thinking up ideas."

Brett Marks was standing in line ahead of them. He turned around with a grin on his face.

"You guys are wasting your time. That first prize is as good as mine."

"What are you talking about?" Chet demanded. "You're not so hot in science."

"Both my parents are scientists. I know they'll help me come up with an amazing project."

Chet and Frank exchanged a glance. They didn't want Brett to win the first prize.

"I was in a science fair back home in California," Billy said.

"What was your project on—earthquakes?" Zack dug Brett in the ribs.

"That must have been easy for him to demonstrate." Brett chuckled. "He just had to walk up and down the room and ker-boom—instant earthquake!" Brett laughed hard at his own joke. "Hey, that's what we should call him—Earthquake Magee!"

"Good name," Zack yelled. "Earthquake Magee. I like it!"

"That's not funny, you guys," Chrissy Parker said. "He just got here. Be nice."

"Don't listen to those guys, Billy," Chet said. "Go ahead and make something fantastic for the science fair. That will show them."

"Oh, don't worry about me," Billy said. "I'll find a way to get even."

He stepped forward and kicked the ball. The ball flew across the schoolyard.

"Hey, that's some foot you've got there!" Frank exclaimed.

"Yeah, my brothers are football players," Billy said. "They've been teaching me since I was a little kid. Just wait until we're in high school and I get to tackle Zack!"

He grinned at Frank and Chet. Billy's okay, Frank thought. I don't need to keep an eye on him. He can look after himself.

2

Whose Idea Was It?

After school that day Frank and Joe walked home with Chet and Billy.

"Hey, you guys," Chet said. "I think I've come up with a great project for the science fair."

"You've invented that miracle food you were talking about? Great taste, fills you up, and no calories?"

"No, but almost as good." Chet grinned happily. "I checked a book out of the library. It tells how to make a hot-dog cooker using solar power. Next time we go camping I won't have to wait for my dad to fire up the barbecue. I'll just open up my solar-powered cooker. Then I can cook hot dogs any time I want."

"Cool," Joe said, "or should I say hot?"

"As long as it's not raining," Frank pointed out.

"What about you guys?" Chet asked.

"I might do what I did in California," Billy said. "But I'm going to ask my big brothers for ideas, too. They've been in a ton of science fairs."

"You've got big brothers?" Joe asked.

"Yeah, three. One in college, one in high school, and one in junior high," Billy said. "I'm the shrimp of the family."

The other boys laughed. "Some shrimp," Frank said.

"You should see my brother Mike," Billy said. "He plays college football. He's huge! He really does make the room shake when he comes in."

"Have you decided what you're going to do for the science fair yet?" Chet asked the Hardy brothers.

"I've got a great idea," Frank said.

"What is it?" Billy asked.

"It's a secret for now. I've got to work on it first."

"I've got a great idea," Joe said. "Mine's a secret, too."

The Hardy boys waved goodbye at the end of the street, then they walked home together.

"What's so secret about your idea?" Joe asked Frank.

"You'll see," Frank said. "What's so secret about yours?"

"You'll see," Joe said. He ran up the front steps ahead of Frank. "Hi, Mom, we're home," he yelled. He dropped his book bag in the front hall. "Guess what? We're having a science fair and the parents can come and see it!"

"How exciting," Mrs. Hardy said. "Do you know what you're going to do yet?"

"Sort of," Joe said.

"Sort of," Frank said.

* * *

When Mr. Hardy came home from his work at the detective agency, the family sat down to dinner.

"Dad," Frank said. "We're having a science fair at school, and I want you to help me with my idea."

"Sure, son. I'll be glad to," Mr. Hardy said. "What is it?"

"I'm going to show how detectives use science to catch crooks," Frank said. "And I need you to show me what you do."

Joe's mouth opened in horror. "No way!" he yelled. "That was *my* idea for the science fair. You stole it from me!"

Frank glared at his brother. "I did not! I came up with it first!"

"Did not!" Joe said.

"Did too!" Frank yelled back.

"That's enough, boys," Mr. Hardy said firmly. "We do not yell at the dinner table."

"But it was my idea, Dad—" Joe began.

Mr. Hardy held up his hand. "I'm going to settle this very easily," he said. "You both came up with the same idea because it was an easy one for you—I'm a detective. But you can both forget it."

"Dad!" Frank and Joe exclaimed.

"I'm not lending either of you my detecting tools and secrets," Mr. Hardy said.

"Why not?" Frank demanded.

"A science fair shouldn't be just show and tell," Mr. Hardy said. "It should be your own experiments. It's a good chance to try out something new to see if it works. If you want to do projects about detective work, fine—but think up your own projects I'm not doing your work for you."

After dinner Frank went into Joe's room. "I'm sorry I yelled," he said.

"Me, too," Joe said. "I guess it's pretty obvious why we came up with the same idea."

"So, what do we do now?" Frank asked. "Mrs. Burton wants us to tell her about our ideas tomorrow."

"I brought home these books," Joe said.

They sat on his bed and looked through them. "This is neat." Frank pointed at the page. "It's a viewer that lets you spy around corners. That could be useful for a detective."

"Hey, that looks like fun," Joe said.

"You can make it if you want, Joe."

"But what about you?" Joe asked.

"I'm just getting an idea," Frank said. "I'd like to do something with fingerprints. You know how no two prints are the same? I wonder if prints look alike in families?"

"That's a great idea, Frank," Joe said. "Ask Dad. He'll know."

"No, I'm going to get lots of fingerprints and see for myself," Frank said. "That way it's a real experiment."

The next day Mrs. Burton asked the fourth grade about their science-fair projects. There were a lot of good ideas. Some kids were going to grow plants under different conditions. Some were doing experiments with the five senses. Some were building models. Frank told about his fingerprints.

"Billy?" Mrs. Burton asked.

"I'm going to make candy from a glass of water," Billy said.

Zack and Brett started laughing.

"Candy from a glass of water!" Zack spluttered.

"Boy, Earthquake, what a wimpy idea," Brett said.

Mrs. Burton frowned at them. "There are no wimpy ideas in science," she said. "Sometimes really small things have led to great discoveries. Who would have thought that growing mold in a dish would lead to penicillin? So, no more remarks about any of these projects, okay?"

She waited until Brett nodded. "What about you, Brett?" Mrs. Burton asked.

"I'm going to build a seismograph," Brett said proudly.

"What's that?" some other kids asked.

"It's an instrument to measure earthquakes," Brett said. "Just in case we have one in the classroom."

Mrs. Burton was still frowning. "Are you

serious about this, Brett, or are you just trying to be mean to Billy?"

"No, I'm serious," Brett said. "I got the idea because of Billy, but I'm building a real seismograph. It will really work."

Mrs. Burton shook her head. "That sounds like a big project for a fourth grader."

"No problem," Brett said. He looked pleased with himself.

He knows his parents will help him build it, Frank thought. If Brett won with a project his parents built it wouldn't be a science fair anymore—it would be a science unfair!

3

Science Un-fair!

Wow, look at all this stuff, Frank," Joe murmured to his brother as they carried their projects into the auditorium. It was two weeks later, the day of the science fair. "I don't think I'm going to win anything with my spyscope."

"Maybe not," Frank said. "But at least you know you made it yourself. Some of these projects look as if parents did most of the work." He nudged Joe. "Take a look at Brett's seismograph. I bet his parents made it."

There were long tables around the walls of the auditorium. Each table had a name on it. Mrs. Burton's class had been given tables on the far wall, next to Joe's class. Brett was setting up a fantastic model on an empty table. It looked like a very thin toy crane. A pen hung down from the long arm, just touching a drum with paper wrapped around it.

"How does that work, Brett?" Joe asked.

"Simple. When there's an earthquake, the table shakes. The pen moves from side to side. The drum turns and the pen makes squiggles that show how bad the earthquake is."

"How does the drum turn?" Frank asked.

Brett shrugged. "Rubber bands and things. It's kind of complicated."

Yeah, and your parents built it, Frank thought.

Frank found a place at the end of Brett's table and opened up his display of fingerprints. He had taken prints from six families as well as his whole class. It did seem

that his prints and Joe's prints were kind of alike. So were Chet's and his sister Iola's.

"Hey, Frank, you have to see this," Joe called.

Joe pointed to a toy robot on the next table. "Look what Mike Mendez made."

"A toy robot?" Frank asked.

"Nah. It's a real burglar alarm. He used the robot body so that burglars wouldn't guess. Isn't it neat?"

Mike smiled shyly. "It sends out a photo-electric beam. If anyone breaks the beam, it sets off a siren and a camera takes a picture of the intruder."

"I bet it doesn't really work," Brett sneered. "You just joined up a lot of wires and bells and dumb stuff to make it look good."

"We'll see if it works when we show our projects to the judges," Mike said.

"What are you talking about? Do we have to do that?" Brett asked.

"Sure. Didn't you know?" Mike asked. "After lunch everyone has to explain what they've made and demonstrate how it works."

"You'd better pray for an earthquake after lunch, Brett," Frank said.

"I'll just get Magee to walk past," Brett said. He moved away from Frank and Joe. "Hey, Earthquake," he called. "Let's see what you're doing there."

Billy's project was just a glass of water with an ice-cream stick lying across the top. A string was dangling from the ice-cream stick into the water.

Brett burst into phony laughter. "Is that it? What a loser," he sneered. "And don't go near my seismograph, you hear? I don't want you setting it off too soon. It's very delicate, you know."

At lunch recess that day a cold wind was blowing. It was about to rain.

"Hey, no fair. How am I going to demonstrate a solar-powered cooker when there's no sun?" Chet demanded. "Lucky I cooked some hot dogs yesterday. I can show the judges those."

"I wish you had a cooker going right

now, Chet," Joe said. "I'm freezing out here."

"Me, too," Chet said. "I think I'm going inside to get my scarf. This wind is too much."

"Yooowwww!" Zack and Brett and their friends ran past, making airplane noises and knocking off Joe's cap as they ran.

"Knock it off, you guys," Joe yelled after them.

"We already did!" Zack yelled back, laughing.

"Weirdos!" Chet yelled after them. He watched them run around the schoolyard, annoying people.

Chrissy Parker and her friends were huddled close to the building, out of the wind, playing with Working Wendy dolls. Chrissy had Lawyer Laurie, the latest doll in the series. Zack and Brett ran up to them.

"Oh, look what I've got!" Brett yelled. He snatched up one of the dolls. "Oh, help me! I'm being kidnapped!" he yelled in a high, doll-like voice as he danced away.

"Give it back!" Chrissy tried to catch him.

Brett laughed and held the doll up high, out of her reach.

Just as Frank and Joe were going over to help her, Chrissy snatched the doll back from Brett. "You jerk," she said. "I'm going to put my doll away in my cubby right now, and you guys are going to be sorry!"

She stalked around the corner in the direction of the front entrance.

"Now you're going to get it, Brett," Zack muttered. "She's going to tell on you."

"Tattletale." Brett grumbled. He watched Chrissy go, then ran after her.

"You want to shoot some hoops?" Frank asked Joe.

Joe shook his head. "My fingers are too cold to hold the ball."

"Hey, Billy, where are you going?" Frank called as Billy passed them.

"Some kid told me I'm wanted in the office," Billy said. He hurried past them.

"Oh, good, there's the bell," Joe said. "Time to go in and unfreeze."

27

But when they got to the front steps the teacher on yard duty stopped them. "Recess isn't over yet," she said.

"But we heard the bell," Joe told her.

She looked at her watch. "You made a mistake. You've got five more minutes."

Joe turned away, puzzled. "I'm sure I heard a bell, aren't you, Frank?"

"I thought so," Frank said.

Billy and Chet came back out to join them.

"Where's your scarf, Chet?" Frank asked.

"My scarf? Oh, I forgot it," Chet said.

"But that's what you went in for," Frank reminded him.

Chet laughed awkwardly. "Oh, yeah. It was, wasn't it?"

Just then the bell rang loud and clear, and they filed inside.

Later that afternoon the third and fourth graders marched excitedly into the auditorium.

"Wait quietly beside your exhibits,

please," Ms. Vaughn, the principal, said. "And please don't touch anything. It might take a while for the judges to get to you."

Frank went to stand at the table beside his fingerprints. Brett walked past him. Suddenly he froze. "Oh no! I don't believe it!" he yelled. "After all my hard work. It's ruined."

Everyone turned to look. The seismograph was lying smashed to pieces, half on the table, half on the floor. Next to it Mike's burglar alarm also lay smashed. Who could have done such a terrible thing?

4

The Hardys Find a Clue

I thought I heard the bell on my burglar alarm going off during lunch recess," Mike said angrily. "Now I know why, and I want to know who."

Joe felt sick to his stomach. He knew how hard Mike had worked on his project. He knew it would have won a prize for sure.

Mrs. Burton came over to look at both ruined projects. Ms. Vaughn was with her.

"This is horrible," Ms. Vaughn said angrily. "Someone has deliberately wrecked these projects. Believe me, Brett and Mike, we will find out who did this!"

"I know who did it," Brett said.

The students had been whispering excitedly. Now they were silent, staring at Brett.

"Who else?" Brett went on. "It was Billy Magee. I saw him go into the building during lunch recess. He wanted to get back at me because I had been teasing him."

"But why would he wreck Mike's project, too?" Frank asked. "He doesn't even know Mike."

"I bet I know what happened," Zack said. He came to stand beside Brett's project. "Earthquake came in here and knocked the stuff over by mistake. Everyone knows how clumsy he is."

"That is a very serious accusation," Ms. Vaughn said. "Let's hear what Billy has to say."

Mrs. Burton looked at Billy. His freckled face was bright red.

"Is any of this true, Billy?" she asked quietly. "Did you come in here at lunchtime?"

"I—I came into the building, yes, but—" Billy stammered.

"See! I knew it!" Brett exclaimed.

"Did you come in here and knock over these projects?" Mrs. Burton went on. "If it was an accident we'll understand, but we have to know the truth."

"No!" Billy looked around the room. "I didn't even come in here. I came inside because some kid told me I was wanted in the office."

"Who told you?" Brett demanded.

Billy looked around. "Some kid I didn't know. A little kid—first grader maybe? He came up to me and said I had to go to the office right away."

"What for?" Mrs. Burton asked.

Billy shrugged. "It was a mistake. The secretary said she hadn't sent anyone to find me."

"Hah!" Zack sneered. "Nice try, Earthquake. Great excuse. Why don't you just own up? You know you did it!"

"That's enough, Zack," Mrs. Burton said

sternly. "We have no proof that Billy did this. A person is innocent until proven guilty, you know."

Ms. Vaughn held up her hand. "I think we should all go back to our classrooms," she said. "We need time to find out more about this. Maybe we should put off the judging until tomorrow. I hope we can get to the bottom of this mystery very soon. Please line up at the doors with your teachers."

Billy just stood there, staring. He looked as if he was in shock. Chet and Frank grabbed his arms. "Come on, Billy," Chet said. "Let's go."

Billy glared at Brett and Zack. "They've made everyone think I did it, Frank," he said. "How can I prove that I'm innocent?"

"I'll try to help you, Billy," Frank said.

He ran over to find Joe, who was lining up with Mrs. Adair's class. "Joe, we've got to stay to look for clues," he said. "See if your teacher will let you help Mike pick up the pieces."

"Good idea," Joe said. He went up to

Mike. "Do you want me to help you pick up this mess?" he asked. "Maybe your burglar alarm can be fixed."

"I doubt it," Mike said, "but thanks anyway, Joe. It's worth a try."

"Then let's ask Mrs. Adair," Joe said. They went up to the third-grade teacher. She listened to Mike and nodded. "Of course you can stay, Mike. I feel bad for you. I know how hard you worked."

"And can I help him?" Joe asked quickly.

Mrs. Adair smiled at him. "All right, Joe. You're being a kind friend."

Joe wanted to help Mike, but he also wanted a chance to look for clues.

He saw that Frank was asking his teacher the same thing. The other students filed out of the auditorium. Soon just Frank, Joe, Mike, and Brett were left. They went back to look at the smashed projects.

"I'm sorry your project got damaged, Mike," Brett said. "I'll help you fix it, if you want."

"Thanks, Brett. But I don't think it can be

fixed. What about yours?" Mike sounded surprised.

Frank was surprised, too. How come bratty Brett was being so nice to a third grader?

"Mine can't be fixed either," Brett said, kneeling down beside it. "Look at it. It's in a zillion pieces." He shook his head. "I don't get it. If Earthquake was mad at me, I can understand it. But he didn't even know you."

"We don't know that Billy did it," Frank said quickly.

"Face it, Hardy," Brett snapped. "Who else would want to do something like this?"

"There's only one way to find out," Frank said. He went over to his own exhibit and came back with a bottle of talcum powder and some sticky tape.

"What are you doing?" Brett asked.

"Looking for fingerprints," Frank said. "I already have the fingerprints of our whole class on my project board. We can easily see if Billy's fingerprints are on any of the pieces here. See—I'm going to sprinkle the powder on the surface, then blow it away. Next I brush lightly and the pattern of fingerprints shows. Then I press on the sticky tape and—ta da! The fingerprint comes off."

Brett snorted. "Stop playing at detective, Hardy. Just because your dad is a detective doesn't mean that you can really find clues." He picked up a handful of pieces and dumped them on the table. "I'm getting out of here. There's nothing more I can do."

Frank watched Brett leave the auditorium.

"I guess I'll have to go back to my classroom soon," he said. "But I'm going to take fingerprints first. Maybe they'll show us who smashed this stuff."

Joe had been squatting next to Mike, picking up pieces of Mike's burglar alarm that had fallen on the floor. Suddenly he gave a cry and pounced on something.

"What is it?" Frank asked. "Have you found something, Joe?"

Joe nodded. He opened his hand. In it lay a shoe—a very, very small shoe that could belong only to a doll.

5

Who Is the Smasher?

"Wait a second!" Frank exclaimed. "Chrissy Parker and her friends were playing with dolls today."

"And remember Chrissy got mad and took her doll inside?" Joe said. "She could have come in here and wrecked both Brett's and Mike's projects."

"But why?" Mike asked.

"Maybe it was to get back at Brett for teasing her and taking her doll away," Joe suggested.

Frank shook his head. "I don't think so.

38

Chrissy isn't mean. And anyway, she wasn't mad at Mike."

"Then maybe she wanted to win first prize herself," Joe said.

Frank hesitated. He remembered that Chrissy was the one who said she never had a chance to win when the science fair was for the whole school. Maybe Chrissy did want to win very badly. But he couldn't imagine Chrissy doing anything like this. It just wasn't like her.

"I don't think she would do this," he said. "Somebody had to be very angry to do this. These projects are smashed to pieces."

"Let's look for more clues," Joe said. "We might not have much more time here."

"I'll do more fingerprinting," Frank said. "You two go on searching."

"Oh no!" Joe exclaimed.

"What?" Frank and Mike looked up.

"Down here on the floor," Joe said. "Do you see what I see?"

Frank and Mike saw that Joe was pointing at a trail of crumbs. Joe bent down, picked up a crumb, and sniffed at it.

"They're chip crumbs, Frank," Joe said. "Smells like Nacho cheese flavor. Billy and Chet were both eating chips at lunchtime."

"And we know that Billy went into the building," Mike reminded them. "He said he was told to go to the office."

"And Chet went into the building to get his scarf," Frank said in a puzzled voice. "And he came out again without it." Then he shook his head. "But Chet's our friend. He would never do a mean thing like this."

"Then why did he say he was going to get his scarf?" Joe asked. "What was he doing in here?"

"It's just possible that he decided to get back at Brett for teasing Billy," Frank said. "But he would never smash Mike's project."

"So it had to be Billy after all," Joe said quietly. "He was eating chips. He had plenty of reasons to get back at Brett. And he did tell us that he was going to get even someday."

"Can you really believe that?" Frank asked. "But maybe Zack was right for once.

Billy could have come in here and knocked over the projects by accident. He is very clumsy, we know that."

"And then he was too scared to admit it," Joe added. "We should try talking to him. Maybe he'll tell us the truth."

"Okay, I've got some fingerprints," Frank said. He stood up, holding a strip of sticky tape. "Let's take them over to my board to see how they match up."

Mike was trying to put the pieces of his burglar alarm back together. He held the robot head in one hand and the body in the other. Wires were sticking out in all directions.

"Do you think you can fix it?" Joe asked.

Mike shook his head. "I don't think so," he said. "Whoever smashed this really demolished it."

Joe walked over to Frank. "Any luck?" he asked.

Frank was holding up the piece of tape and checking the fingerprints against the prints on the board.

"Nothing," Frank said. "The only finger-prints I've found on Brett's seismograph are Brett's own."

"That doesn't really mean anything," Joe said. "If Billy bumped into the table, he wouldn't have touched the seismograph with his fingers. And someone could have smashed it with a stick or something."

Frank nodded. "That's true, Joe. And most kids were wearing gloves at lunchtime, too, so they wouldn't have left any prints."

"Where do we go from here?" Joe asked. "I guess Chrissy and Chet and Billy are still all suspects."

They jumped as Mike let out a big shriek.

"What? What is it?" Joe demanded.

"Look at this!" Mike shouted. "My burglar alarm might be smashed, but the camera inside it is still okay. Lucky it was in the robot's head. If it worked properly, it might have taken a picture of the kid who smashed it."

6

Picture This!

After school Frank waited for Joe outside the front entrance.

"Don't go home yet," he said. "We have to stay to interview the suspects. That's what Dad would do if he wanted to solve this case."

"Good idea," Joe said. "And if one of them won't talk to us, then we'll know who might have done it."

Joe looked up as Chet came running through the door. He stopped and smiled when he saw the Hardy brothers. "Oh, there you are. I thought you guys had gone without me."

Frank glanced at Joe. He didn't know how he was going to tell Chet that he was one of the suspects.

"I hurried out because I wanted to talk to some kids," he said.

"What about?" Chet asked.

"About the science fair," Frank said.

"Yeah, Chet, we're going to find out who smashed Brett's and Mike's projects," Joe added.

"Great," Chet said. "Let me know if I can help. It's not fair that everyone thinks it's Billy. You don't really think he did it, do you?"

"Not on purpose," Frank said. "But it could have been an accident and now he's too scared to own up."

"I don't think Billy is a scaredy-cat," Chet said. "And I'm pretty sure he didn't go into the auditorium."

"Oh?" Frank asked. "How do you know that?"

45

"Because . . . because he said he didn't and that's good enough for me," Chet said quickly.

Frank glanced at Joe. Chet sounded as if he was flustered. Could their suspicions be right after all?

At that moment Chrissy Parker came out of the building with her friends.

"Hold on a moment, Chet," Frank said. "We have to talk to Chrissy."

"She's not a suspect, is she?" Chet asked loudly.

Frank frowned at him. He wanted to catch Chrissy by surprise. Luckily she was too busy talking and laughing with her friends to have heard Chet.

Frank went over to her and tapped her arm. "Can I talk to you for a moment, please?"

Chrissy looked surprised. "What about?"

"The science fair," Frank said. "We're trying to solve the mystery."

Chrissy grinned. "Oh, right. The world-famous detectives!"

Joe came and stood beside Frank. "We know that you went into the building at lunchtime," he said.

"So? I went to put my doll in my cubby."

"We thought you might have seen something," Joe said.

"What kind of thing?"

"Somebody creeping into the auditorium?" Frank suggested.

Chrissy shook her head. "I didn't see anybody. I put my dolls back, and then I came straight out again."

"Do you have your Lawyer Laurie doll with you now?" Joe asked.

"Yes." Chrissy looked surprised.

"May we see it?" Joe went on.

"What for?" Chrissy looked over at her friends. "Listen, I have to go. Sorry I can't help you guys."

Joe held out his hand with the tiny shoe in it. "Is your doll missing a shoe?" he asked.

"Where did you find that?" Chrissy demanded. She looked worried now.

"In the auditorium, right beside the two smashed exhibits," Joe said.

"Look, I can explain," Chrissy said quickly. "I was going past the auditorium to my room. The door was open. I looked inside, and I saw that the sign on the top of my board had slipped sideways. I knew the judging was this afternoon, so I ran in and put the sign straight again."

"And what about Brett's and Mike's projects?" Frank asked.

"I didn't touch them. They were fine when I left."

"Thanks, Chrissy," Frank said. "You've been a big help. At least we know it happened toward the end of lunch hour."

"We must have heard the bell from Mike's burglar alarm, remember?" Joe exclaimed. "We thought recess was over, but the yard-duty teacher said we still had five minutes to go. That means the projects were destroyed five minutes before the end of recess."

"And you didn't pass anybody in the halls?" Frank asked Chrissy.

"I told you, no," Chrissy said. "But I saw Billy in the office. Now I really have to go. Sorry."

She ran to join her friends.

Joe looked at Frank. "So Billy was still inside when Chrissy went out again. He would have had a chance to go into the auditorium before the end of recess."

"Here he is now," Frank said. "I don't want to do this, but we have to."

He ran and grabbed Billy. Billy's face broke into a big smile. "Oh, hi, Frank. Have you managed to find out who really did smash Brett's seismograph?"

"Not yet," Frank said, "but we're getting closer. Why don't you tell us again exactly what you did at lunchtime."

Billy wrinkled his nose as if he was thinking hard. "I was in the schoolyard with you guys," he said. "Then a little kid came up to me and said I had to go to the office."

"Did he know your name?" Joe asked. "How did he know it was you?"

Billy shrugged. "I didn't ask. I just went."

"And?" Joe prompted.

"I got to the office, and they said I'd made a mistake. They didn't want to see me. So I came out again."

"And you didn't go near the auditorium?" Frank asked.

"Why would I want to?" Billy demanded. "You know I would never do a rotten thing like that."

"Brett's been mean to you," Frank said. "You might have wanted to get back at him."

"And you did say you were going to get even someday," Joe reminded him.

"I didn't mean like that," Billy said. He grinned. "I said it because that's what my big brother tells me. He says you wait until you tackle those guys on the football field. They'll wonder what hit them. He's a star football player in college. So I think of that every time anyone is mean to me."

"When you came out of the office, what did you do?" Joe asked. "Did you see anybody in the halls?"

"Only Chet," Billy said. "He and I came out of the building together."

Frank and Joe turned to look at Chet.

"Yes, Chet," Frank said. "You went in to get your scarf, and you came out without it."

"I know. That was dumb, wasn't it?" Chet attempted to laugh.

"And do you know what we found in the auditorium, right beside the smashed projects?" Joe asked. "We found a trail of chip crumbs. Nacho cheese chips like you were eating, Chet."

Chet looked hurt and astonished. "You guys don't think that I did it, do you?"

"I don't want to think that you did it, Chet," Frank said. "But what were you doing in the auditorium then?"

"Look, I—I can explain," Chet stammered. "But it's kind of embarrassing. That's why I kept quiet."

Frank, Joe, and Billy were all staring at him. Chet blushed. "Okay. If you really want to know, I was still hungry after lunch. Then I remembered the hot dogs on my solar hot-dog cooker. There were three cooked dogs. I decided that I didn't need three for my demonstration. So, I sneaked in and ate one of them."

"Were the projects already smashed when you went past them?" Frank asked.

Chet shook his head. "I don't know. I was too busy eating. I didn't notice."

"Chet, you're hopeless sometimes." Frank sighed.

"Sorry," Chet said.

They started to walk toward the school gate.

"So, now we're no closer to solving the mystery," Frank said. "No fingerprints. We've talked to the only kids we saw going inside the building, and they all had good reasons for being there."

"I wish I had been using my spyscope," Joe said. "I could have peeked around corners and seen someone sneaking into the auditorium. But it's too late now."

* * *

Frank and Joe had just gotten home when the phone rang.

"It's for you, Joe," Laura Hardy called. "It's your friend Mike Mendez."

Joe ran to take the phone call.

"Guess what, Joe, I was right," Mike yelled. "The camera part of my burglar alarm was okay. My brother is helping me develop the picture it took. As soon as it's ready, I'll bring it over to your house. It might show us who smashed my alarm!"

7

The Shiny Sleeve

Frank and Joe waited impatiently until they saw Mike riding his bike down their street. They ran to meet him.

"Well?" Joe asked. "Where is it? Can you see who did it?"

"Not exactly," Mike said. He handed them a fuzzy black-and-white photo.

"This doesn't tell us much at all," Joe said. "It's only a picture of a hand."

"It tells us a couple of things," Mike said. "Whoever smashed my alarm did it on purpose. That hand is about to hit it."

"You're right," Frank said. He examined the picture more carefully. "And we can also see a jacket cuff. Too bad the picture is in black and white. If we knew what color the jacket was, that would be a good clue."

"The cuff could be from any old jacket," Mike said, "but look in the corner there. You can just see some of the jacket above the cuff. See how shiny the fabric is?"

"Yeah, kind of silky," Frank agreed.

"Yeah," Joe said. "So it had to be a girl's jacket, right? Boys don't wear shiny stuff." His face lit up. "Chrissy Parker! I knew her story was too good to be true, and she was wearing a silky jacket yesterday."

"Shiny pink," Frank said. "I know this is a black-and-white picture, but that jacket is definitely not pink."

"And boys do wear shiny stuff," Mike said. "What about football jackets?"

"Oh yeah, right," Joe said. He peered at the photo again. "It does look like the kind of jacket that pro footballers wear."

"Then I know who did it," Frank said sadly. "Billy always wears an Oakland Raiders jacket. It's shiny and black."

"Call him up," Mike said. "Maybe he'll own up now we've got proof."

Frank shook his head. "I'd rather wait until tomorrow," he said. "This isn't something you can do over the phone. His face will tell us whether he's guilty or not."

"It has to be him," Mike said. "All the evidence points to him, doesn't it? He went into the building. We know he's clumsy. We know he has a grudge against Brett, and he wears a shiny black jacket. What more do you want?"

"Nothing, I guess," Frank said. "But I'm sad about it. I like Billy. He's a neat guy."

"Maybe it was an accident," Joe said. "I can understand that he was scared to own up. We can help him."

"That was no accident." Mike waved the picture at them. "Look at that hand coming at my burglar alarm. That is not an accidental hand."

"And it's a pretty big hand, too," Joe added. "Billy has huge hands."

"Okay, we'll talk to him in the morning," Frank said. "Meet us at school, Mike, and bring the picture with you."

Frank didn't sleep well that night. What if Billy wouldn't own up? He knew that Billy was going to get in big, big trouble, and he hated to be the one who told on him. Nobody liked tattletales.

"I just hope that Billy will go to the principal on his own," he said to Joe the next morning. "I don't want to tell on him."

"I know," Joe agreed. "I'd hate to tell on someone."

"Wait up, you guys," Chet yelled. He ran down the street to join them. "What's with you this morning? How come you look so gloomy? There isn't a math test I don't know about, is there?"

"No, we're worried about Billy," Frank said. "Mike's burglar alarm took a photo. It's a picture of a hand about to smash it. It looked like the guy was wearing a shiny and silky, dark jacket."

"Billy wears an Oakland Raiders jacket," Chet said. "That's shiny and black."

Frank nodded. "I know. It really looks as if he did it, Chet."

"Too bad," Chet said. "I like Billy. Any guy who likes Nacho cheese chips is okay with me."

"I like him, too," Frank said. "He got a rough start here thanks to Zack and Brett making fun of him. Now everyone will hate him. He might even get suspended or expelled."

"But if he really smashed those two projects, that was a pretty mean thing to do," Chet pointed out.

Frank sighed. "Well, we have to talk to him. Let's find him and get it over with."

They saw Mike waiting for them at the school gate.

"Billy hasn't arrived yet," he said. "I've got the photo right here."

"Okay, let's stand over by the door,"

Frank said. "We don't want to embarrass Billy at the front gate, where everyone can see us."

They went to stand on one side. Chrissy Parker and her friends arrived. Chrissy was wearing the silky pink jacket, but it had fake fur around the cuffs.

Then finally Billy came in through the gate.

"Hi, guys," he called, and waved to them. He looked relaxed and happy.

Frank took a deep breath. "Billy. Can you come over here a second?"

Billy came over to them. "Hey, Chet. My mom bought a new brand of chips. You want to try some?"

"Not now, Billy," Chet said.

Billy looked at their faces. "What's up?"

"We think we know who smashed those science projects," Frank said.

"You do? Hey, good going," Billy said. "Who was it?"

"It was you, Billy," Frank said. "I feel really bad about this because we're your friends. We'll help you go to the principal, if you like."

Billy's face flushed bright red. "Look, guys, I've told you a zillion times. I didn't do it. I didn't go near the auditorium. I swear it. What do I have to say to make you believe me?"

"Then how do you explain this?" Frank handed him the photo.

"You're the only one who wears a black shiny jacket," Joe said.

"But this photo is black and white," Billy pointed out. "The jacket could be any dark color. Other kids wear football jackets, you know."

"That's true," Frank said. "But what other kid was wearing a football jacket that day *and* went into the auditorium during lunchtime?"

"Let's hang around here by the gate and watch," Chet said. "We can see if any other third or fourth graders are wearing dark shiny jackets."

"Nobody in my class wears a football

jacket," Joe said. He looked at Mike and Mike nodded.

"It's usually older kids," Mike said.

They stood outside the front door and watched students going in.

Right before the bell rang Zack and his buddies arrived. They saw Billy standing there.

"Hey, Earthquake! Smashed any science fairs today?" Zack demanded.

"Yeah, Earthquake, you're in big trouble," Brett growled. "You wrecked my chance to win the science fair."

"It wasn't me!" Billy began. "I keep on telling—"

While he was talking, Joe nudged Frank. He pointed at Brett.

Brett was wearing a dark blue New York Giants jacket.

8

Science . . . Fair!

Frank stared at Brett, then looked back to Joe. He shook his head. "No. It's impossible. Why would he want to wreck his own project? He probably would have won."

"But remember only his fingerprints were on his project?" Joe said. "And he followed Chrissy Parker into the building, didn't he?"

"That's right," Chet said. "I saw him coming in. That was after I'd eaten my hot dog."

Frank stepped forward. "Just a minute, Brett. Before you start accusing people, we'd like to ask you some questions."

A sneer spread across Brett's face. "Playing detective again, huh, Hardy? Give it a break. Just because your dad's a detective doesn't mean that you are. You don't have a clue."

"As a matter of fact we've got several clues," Frank said, "including this one."

He held up the photo for Brett to see.

"What's that?" Brett asked suspiciously.

"Remember that you told Mike his burglar alarm would never work? Well, it did. It took a picture of the person who smashed it. Mike developed that picture last night."

"Let me see that!" Brett made a grab at the photo. Frank jerked it out of his reach. "You can't prove anything!" Brett yelled.

"Oh, no? A hand about to smash the project isn't proof?" Frank demanded. "Someone wearing your jacket, Brett? And there were no fingerprints on your project except your own. Not even smeared fingerprints where someone else knocked it over. That means that nobody touched it except you!"

Brett's face had gone very white. Everyone was staring at him.

"Did you do it, Brett?" Zack asked.

"Do you really want someone else to get blamed for what you did, Brett?" Joe added.

"Okay, so I did it," Brett snapped. "I saw this neat diagram of a seismograph in a science book. It was pretty complicated, but I thought my parents would help me make it. They're both scientists, you know. They can do stuff like that."

He looked down at his feet and kicked his toe against the pavement.

"But when I told my parents about it, they said I had to do it myself or it wouldn't be a learning experience."

"Boy, what jerks!" Zack muttered.

Brett sighed. "I guess I should have known that they wouldn't do it for me. That's just the way they are. Okay, so it was too hard for me. So I just stuck the pieces together to make it look like the picture. It didn't really work."

He looked up again at the faces around him. "I didn't know we were going to have to demonstrate for the judges. When I found that out, I knew they'd see my project was phony. So I crept in and smashed it."

"But why smash Mike's, too?" Chet demanded. "That was so mean."

Brett shrugged. "I was sure I could pin it on Earthquake. Everyone knew he was clumsy. Everyone knew I'd been giving him a hard time. I thought if I knocked two projects over, it would look as if someone clumsy had bumped into the table.

"I told a little kid to go find Earthquake and say he was wanted in the office. Then everyone would see him going into the building. I sneaked in after Chrissy Parker. I never dreamed that stupid burglar alarm would really work. It totally freaked me out when the bell went off."

Brett looked at Mike. "I'm sorry I smashed your project. It was really good. I bet you would have won. Is there any way I can help you rebuild before the judging today?"

Mike shook his head. "No, but thanks for the offer. I'm just glad to know it did what it was supposed to. It's nice when an idea in your head really does work."

"I think you'll grow up to be a scientist or inventor, Mike," Joe said proudly. "I'm going to tell those judges that your alarm worked and you deserve a prize."

He and Mike went in through the front door. Frank turned to Brett, "Are you going to tell the principal?"

"I think I'll tell Mrs. Burton first," Brett said. "She's not so scary." He went over to Billy. "I'm sorry, Earthquake," he said.

That afternoon the third and fourth graders explained their projects to the judges. The next morning Mrs. Burton's class went back to the auditorium to see who had won. Frank's project had an honorable-mention ribbon on it. So did Chet's hot-dog cooker.

"All right!" Chet said. He gave Frank a high five.

They were both smiling as they walked past the remains of Mike's burglar alarm.

"Hey, look!" Chet exclaimed. He pointed at a first-place blue ribbon. "Mike won after all!"

Mrs. Burton came to stand behind them. "Mike still had all the plans for his alarm, and he showed us how the alarm worked. We thought it was a very clever invention—most original."

"I bet Mike is pleased," Frank said. "The Nature Place is his favorite store."

Frank heard a girl exclaim, "Wow, look at this! Billy, this is so cool."

Frank and Chet joined other fourth graders at Billy's project. Yesterday it had just looked like a glass of water with a string dangling in it. Today shiny crystals were starting to grow up and down the string.

"You really did make candy!" Frank exclaimed.

"How did you do it?" Chrissy Parker asked. "It was only water."

"It was water with a whole lot of sugar in it," Billy said. "You have to boil up water with as much sugar as it will take. I had one cup of water and more than one cup of sugar. When all the sugar has dissolved and the mixture has gotten cool again, you pour it into a glass. Then you hang a piece of string in it and the sugar makes crystals along the string."

"That is so neat," Chrissy said. "I'm going to try that."

"Me, too," Chet said. "My own candy factory at home? I love it."

"And you got an honorable mention, too," Frank said. "Way to go, Billy."

"Thanks," Billy mumbled. "And thanks to you guys for sticking by me even when you thought I'd done something pretty bad."

Chet looked at Frank and laughed. "You bet we're your friends, Billy. What a friend to have—one who can make instant candy!"

The Hardy Boys® are:

THE CLUES BROTHERS™

By Franklin W. Dixon

Look for a brand-new story every other month

A <u>MINSTREL</u>® BOOK

Published by Pocket Books

1398-08

THE NANCY DREW NOTEBOOKS®

by Carolyn Keene
Illustrated by Anthony Accardo

Simon & Schuster Mail Order Dept. BWB
200 Old Tappan Rd., Old Tappan, N.J. 07675   A MINSTREL BOOK
Published by Pocket Books

Please send me the books I have checked above. I am enclosing $_____ (please add $0.75 to cover the postage and handling for each order. Please add appropriate sales tax). Send check or money order--no cash or C.O.D.'s please. Allow up to six weeks for delivery. For purchase over $10.00 you may use VISA: card number, expiration date and customer signature must be included.

Name _____

Address _____

City _____ State/Zip _____

VISA Card # _____ Exp.Date _____

Signature _____ 1045-16

Sabrina
The Teenage Witch™

Salem's Tails™

What's it like to be a powerful warlock,
sentenced to one hundred years in a
cat's body for trying to take over the world?

Ask Salem.

**Read all about Salem's magical
adventures in this new series based on the
hit ABC-TV show!**

#1 CAT TV
#2 Teacher's Pet
#3 You're History
#4 The King of Cats
#5 Dog day Afternoon
Salem Goes to Rome

Now available!
Look for a new title every other month

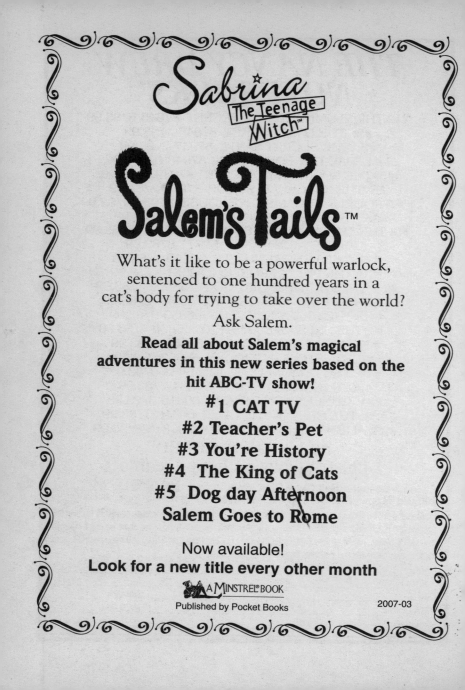
A MINSTREL BOOK
Published by Pocket Books

2007-03